Foreword

Dear Reader,

I am a person who knows what it's like to lose someone I love, feel on the outside of people, and want desperately to fit in. I know what it's like to be anxious and afraid and have my heart broken and feel alone. The wonderful thing about stories like these is that they remind us that there are others out there just like us. They make us know we're not alone.

Always remember: You are the only you that exists in this world. *You are not alone*. And, what's more, you are lovely. You are amazing. You are unique and beautiful and YOU. Know that even when life is darkest, there are bright places everywhere, and you are one of them.

Love,
Jennifer Niven
New York Times bestselling author of *All the Bright Places* and *Holding Up the Universe*

For my siblings, thanks for putting up with all of my **blue days** as a kid.
For those who bought the first book, thank you!
For those who set their life to music, I hope it is a beautiful song.

www.mascotbooks.com

Alycat and the Monday Blues

For more information, please contact:
Mascot Books
560 Herndon Parkway #120
Herndon, VA 20170
info@mascotbooks.com

Library of Congress Control Number: 2017910260

CPSIA Code: PRT0717A
ISBN-13: 978-1-68401-245-9

Printed in the United States

Alycat
and the
Monday Blues

Alysson Foti Bourque
Illustrations by Chiara Civati

Foreword by Jennifer Niven

Alycat headed down the stairs in a slow, unexcited crawl.

How did the weekend fly by so fast? she thought. **It's already Monday.**

"Mom, do I have to go to school today?" Alycat asked. "I don't feel good, and I can't find my shoes." Mom felt Alycat's forehead. "I'm not sick. I just have the **Monday Blues**. And I don't have any talent for the talent show tomorrow."

"Alycat, you'll feel better when you get to school. You'll figure something out for the talent show. You always do," said Mom.

Alycat wasn't convinced but headed to school anyway.

During calendar time, the class helpers were picked for the week. Alycat wanted to be the weather reporter, but Spotty was chosen instead.

"Today will be rainy with blustery winds," Spotty announced. "Hold on to your hats. The rain will be spotty—like me!"

The class laughed, but Alycat didn't join in.

When the bell rang, the kittens headed out into the gloomy weather, led by Luna—the line leader. Alycat stared off into space, daydreaming about the talent show. She imagined her classmates performing while she stood backstage without anything to show.

As the last kitten left the classroom, a few papers were caught by the howling wind and flew outside.

"Oh no! Our artwork!" Alycat yelled.

She chased the papers as fast as she could. When she finally fetched the last one, she was on the other side of the school.

Phew! she thought. *That was a close one!*

Alycat heard a jazzy sound coming from a nearby classroom and peeked inside.

It was Spotty!

"Spotty, that sounds amazing!" called Alycat.

"**Thanks**, I'm practicing my saxophone for the talent show, but I don't have any words for the song."

"Maybe I can help. Play it again, and I'll sing," Alycat said.

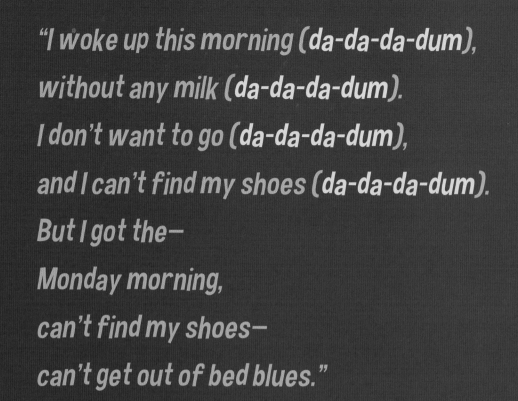

"I woke up this morning (**da-da-da-dum**),
without any milk (**da-da-da-dum**).
I don't want to go (**da-da-da-dum**),
and I can't find my shoes (**da-da-da-dum**).
But I got the—
Monday morning,
can't find my shoes—
can't get out of bed blues."

"Wow!" Spotty yelled. "That was perfect! Do you think you could sing when I play tomorrow?"

"I'd love to!" Alycat said excitedly.

The storm passed, and the clouds cleared. Soon, Alycat and her brother, Bugsy, were on the bus heading home.

"How was your day?" Mom asked as they walked inside.

"Great!" said Bugsy.

"Jazzy!" said Alycat. "I'm going to sing the blues with Spotty in the talent show tomorrow!"

"That sounds great!" said Dad. "I was in the school band and still have my harmonica."

"Really?" Alycat asked. "Will you help us finish our song? Spotty is coming over to practice."

"Sure," said Dad.

Alycat ran upstairs to find the perfect outfit for the talent show. While pulling everything *jazzy* out of her toy box, she daydreamed about every detail that would make the performance spectacular.

When the doorbell rang, Alycat gathered her props to meet Spotty downstairs.

"**Wow!**" said Spotty. "You look **jAzZ-taSTic**, Alycat!"

"Thanks! I found sunglasses and a hat for you to wear, too. Let's turn this **blue day** into a new day!"

Alycat and Spotty practiced for hours on their performance until Spotty's mom called for him to come home.

"See you tomorrow!" said Spotty.

Alycat was so excited she barely slept a wink that night. When she finally closed her eyes, she dreamed about her **rock star** moment with Spotty.

The next day, Alycat ran downstairs with a pep in her step and her sunglasses on.

"Check it out, Mom. Today I'm wearing my **blue suede shoes!**"

"I'm so glad you discovered your hidden talent, Alycat!" Mom exclaimed. "Everybody has something special about them. You just have to try new things to figure out what it is."

"You're right!" Alycat said. "While I was helping Spotty with his song, he helped me figure out my talent!"

"You make a good team," laughed Mom.

The bus driver honked the horn, and Alycat and Bugsy were out the door in a hurry.

At the talent show, Alycat was nervous but excited. Luna finished her fearless gymnastics routine with the most incredible bounces and rolls. Then it was Spotty and Alycat's turn!

Spotty and Alycat took their places. They started their **jazzy** duet, and the other kittens started clapping and dancing!

"I woke up this morning (da-da-da-dum),
without any milk (da-da-da-dum).
I don't want to go (da-da-da-dum),
and I can't find my shoes (da-da-da-dum).
But I got the—
Monday morning,
can't find my shoes—
can't get out of bed blues."

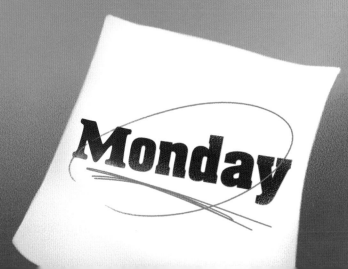

"I woke up at night (*da-da-da-dum*)
in such a fright (*da-da-da-dum*).
I saw a shadow (*da-da-da-dum*),
turned on the light (*da-da-da-dum*).
But I got the—
Monday night,
in such a fright—
I want to get out of my bed blues."

Kittens were singing along, and Spotty ended the song with a saxophone riff that earned a standing ovation!

And the talent show winner is — The Harmonicats!" announced the principal.

Spotty and Alycat jumped for joy and ran to get their trophies.

"Thank you for helping me find my hidden talent, Spotty!" said Alycat.

"Sure thing! And thank you for helping me with my song! Now we are a band!"

"We sure are!" cheered Alycat.

About the Author

Alysson Foti Bourque is the author of the *Rhyme or Reason Travel* series, and the multi-award-winning *Alycat* series. Alysson received a Bachelor of Arts degree in Elementary Education from the University of Louisiana at Lafayette and a law degree from Southern University Law Center in Baton Rouge. After practicing law for six years, Alysson traded in writing trial briefs for writing children's books.

She believes that there is an Alycat in all of us, encouraging our imaginations to guide us through new opportunities and adventures. Look for *Alycat and the Friendship Friday* coming soon!

"I woke up this morning (da-da-da-dum),
without any milk (da-da-da-dum).
I don't want to go (da-da-da-dum),
and I can't find my shoes (da-da-da-dum).
But I got the—
Monday morning,
can't find my shoes—
can't get out of bed blues."

"I woke up this morning (da-da-da-dum),
without any milk (da-da-da-dum).
I don't want to go (da-da-da-dum),
and I can't find my shoes (da-da-da-dum).
But I got the—
Monday morning,
can't find my shoes—
can't get out of bed blues."

"I woke up at night (da-da-da-dum)
in such a fright (da-da-da-dum).
I saw a shadow (da-da-da-dum),
turned on the light (da-da-da-dum).
But I got the—
Monday night,
in such a fright—
I want to get out of my bed blues."